JUVENILE PARABLES

Part - 1

By

Neeti Saharan

Editor

Shweta Batra

Anybook

Published By

Anybook

E-mail : contactanybook@gmail.com

Website : www.anybookpublications.com

Price in India : 250/- INR

Hardcover first published by Anybook in 2024

Copyright © 2024 Neeti Saharan

Printed and bound in India

Cover Design & Typesetting by Anybook

ISBN : 978-93-91571-88-7

INTRODUCTION

My first book, **'It's time to live again'** gave me a new name, 'An Author'. It delt with our day-to-day problems and how to handle them with ease. It motivated us that every moment is the right time to start living again and stop just existing.

Above all, it gave an inspiration to me to keep penning my thoughts.

The second book, **'Stepping into their shoes'** was written to bridge the gap between the two generations. It explained that the differences amongst the generations are mere misunderstandings which grow because they are not clarified by discussion and no attempt is made to find solution unitedly. Being true, helpful and respecting others' point of view gives us the scope to develop cordial relationships and make life a better experience to live today and for the years to come.

The third book, **'Family Crossroute'** was yet another guiding handbook which delt with … whether to be in a joint family or a nuclear family. The book tried to present the pros and cons of both living arrangements along with real life experiences of different people which may guide a person to take up that important decision of life.

ABOUT JUVENILE PARABLES

After completing the third book, the child within me took the front seat. These stories are real stories that helped to improve myself as I lived through the various experiences.

I grew up learning good things from everyone around me. Finding goodness in others and improving myself was and is the true me. Being a learner, I always got into the root of every situation and imbibed the best within me. Goodness attracted me as a child and even now.

One day, I got inspired to jot down my childhood incidents and share the moral values in the form of these stories. I learnt a lot from my relatives, friends and family. The incidents are real but the relation and the names have been changed. These learnings are truly very close to my heart.

The teacher within me wishes the children to be morally strong. This book is a gift to young children who will be ethically right and morally strong in their lives. When they grow, these morals would help them take right decisions in life and be self-guided. Gifting them these morals in the form of short stories is an idea that has organically originated within me.

Being a teacher by heart, I love staying connected towards my goal of contributing to the lives of children to grow up as ethically and morally strong, responsible citizens. I often think as a child and walk out solving many problems in my life …. This simple practice could be a part of everyone – young or old to experience the journey called life.

I pray that our juveniles benefit from these parables. It's only then I feel the effort worth it!

PREFACE

This book is written purely to inculcate moral values in our children who can easily do so by observing and absorbing the good that is happening around them and become a better version of themselves as they live each single day.

Also, to let them be aware that there is no fixed pattern to lead life.

We are all born humans but, unfortunately, we have lost the most important innate value of being human.

Being consistently persuasive as a teacher, I seek ways and means and leave no stone unturned to guide young minds blossom. I wish that every child stays grounded personally and, flies high professionally living a fulfilling life of a human being.

This book will inspire children to realize that there is a lot they can learn from the situations around them.

A progressive approach towards the situations which we, as children consider big problems, could and would help the readers to become problem solvers and go-getters.

This book is just a drop in the ocean of young minds but, I am happy to contribute towards the ideal growth of generations to come. Let us make the roots of our coming generations strong and deep rooted.

ACKNOWLEDGEMENT

Firstly, I thank the Almighty for shaping my life in the best possible way. Every experience gave a beautiful lesson that guided me to keep improving in life. Now, as I got inspired by His blessings to pen down few very important values of life along with the experiences.

I thank my family, relatives, friends, cousins and above all teachers for helping me learn good things from their experiences and teachings.

Even at times, reading would teach me something new. I thank all those who wrote good books to inspire, encourage and guide children.

I thank the little ones in advance who will read this book and benefit in their own little way.

I also thank the readers of my earlier three books who constantly encourage me to keep writing. As always, I thank my mother who brought me up with tender love and inculcated the values in a playful manner. I am still learning to be like her.

My little grandson Prayansh keeps motivating me with his innocent behaviour and I find different ways to empower him with values. His gestures also teach me to get the best solutions with innocence.

I feel great pleasure to acknowledge my husband, Shyam Saharan who has always encouraged me to do something creative in life. I thank my biological children, Akshay and Dhrriti who helped me keep my childhood alive through them. I enjoy everyday being their mother and see them growing into good humans. I also thank my son-in-law, Jayanth and daughter-in-law, Isha for bringing a smile whenever I talk to them and feel blessed to have such loving and cultured humans as our family.

I thank Virendra Desai, who published my first book which helped me establish myself as an 'Author.'

I am obliged to thank my nephew, Krishan who recently read my first book and motivated me to keep motivating others by my writings.

I thank my editor friend Shweta Batra to be my critic and guide. I thank her for helping me to present this book in a way that connects to the parents as well as the juveniles.

I also thank my publishers for guiding me right at all times. Special thanks to 'Blue Butterfly Arts' for accepting my writings and being a part of 'Juvenile Parables' journey. I hope more and more children read this book and learn to become solution finders in life and not get influenced by various vices that they come across around them.

FOR THE JUVENILES

FROM THE AUTHOR

JUVENILE PARABLES is purely written with a hope to have a confident, healthy, morally strong, decision maker, solution finder upcoming generation. This book will surely contribute to your precious life to have righteous and virtuous life. All of you are in one of the best periods of your life. It is just because when the young minds grow, they get confused to analyse between good and bad happening around them. Let us make growing easy with the right kind of inputs at the right time.

You all definitely have the right to a wholesome life.

Remember that there are no short cuts to success and peace. Introspection at a later age can take a right shape only, if your moral values are rightly weaved into the thought process. While reading these stories you will feel that they are a part of your day-to-day life. I am grateful to the Almighty to ignite me with this thought of penning down the parables and sharing the same with you all.

Planting values in your tender minds is the moral duty of the elder generations. The ways can be unusual and innovative.

Love for you all is incomparable as you all are precious gifts from the Almighty.

This initiative will surely initiate a fearless, courageous and ethically right version of yourself. It will guide you to become a good social being and further lead a contended life.

May you all have a blessed, meaningful, progressive, healthy, peaceful and contended life.

These stories are tools in your hands that will strengthen your decision-making ability. Let the moral values be an inseparable part of your life.

Gratitude and good luck to our little champs!!!!!

A good human = A good global citizen

CONTENT

1.

A LITTLE TWEAKING COULD MAKE ALL THE DIFFERENCE

When I was around twelve years of age, I had a classmate named Raju. He was an intelligent boy but, did not study regularly. All the time after school was spent playing.

His parents were really worried about him but did not know how to handle him.

Since both his parents were working there was no one at home to monitor him or make him understand what he was losing on. His parents were really down to earth and always taught him good things whenever they got time. They asked him to pray everyday which he did daily.

Whenever we used to ask him about his studies, he would always say, "I do my daily prayers so, I will pass my exams all the time." Gradually he started becoming more and more negligent about his studies.

Since his parents were busy in their own world, they used to compensate their absence by buying him whatever he demanded. He had so many indoor and outdoor games with him but never took any game seriously. These things were just his excuse for not studying.

One day out of concern my mother asked me, "Why is Raju playing all the time, please ask him to study. Isn't he your friend anymore?

"He believes that he will get good marks because he prays to God everyday. He does not listen to his parents or his teachers" I replied.

Nonetheless, one evening while playing in the nearby park, I went near him and said, "Please start studying Raju, we have our semester exams from next month." At first, he ignored me and did not answer. While coming back from the park I again repeated my statement. He simply laughed and said, "God will help me, do not worry".

This time Raju neither paid attention to his studies in the class nor at home. The course was getting tougher day by day, but he was least bothered. During our semester exams, he had all new pens, pencil box, writing board etc. but not even a single word in his mind that he could write on his answer sheet. He just scribbled whatever came to his mind. Whatever he wrote was not at all sufficient to score few marks. All the exams just went like that! Raju used to pray each day before coming to school but not study at all.

Whenever his parents asked him about his studies, he always assured them that he will pass. His parents trusted him as even they were not demanding very high percentage from their son. They just

Juvenile Parables

wanted him to keep passing in his exams. This time it was different and even passing the exams was too difficult for him.

He did not know anything in his exams.

HE FAILED.

He came back home crying and complaining to his mother, "Look mother I did my prayers everyday but God did not help me. You always said that if we do our prayers sincerely, God hears and fulfils our prayers." His mother was confused and upset with his academic result. When she went to meet his class teacher, she came to know about her son's actual behaviour. She understood what was actually happening in her son's mind.

She very smartly started adding something more to her son's prayers. She said, "Please do not worry my child, God only helps those who help themselves". "Start studying from today along with your prayers and see that you will surely get good marks." He started doing this from that day onwards.

Since Raju was already upset with all the humiliation that he was facing in school, this incident shook him from within. This was an unexpected thing that happened within him for the first time. Maybe the Almighty heard his prayers this time.

That day onwards there was a drastic change in Raju. He was a changed boy now.

Few days later he came to my home and said, "Chutki, will you please help me in my studies?" He very well knew that I always gave my sincere and true suggestions to him. I somehow knew that Raju had the potential to get really good marks if he studies regularly. I quickly said "Sure, why not."

From that day onwards, both of us started studying together

till the time he gained confidence of studying on his own.

It was a great surprise for all of us that Raju was trying to change himself for good. His true potential gradually started showing up.

In the next final exams, my friend Raju came first in class. All of us, including our teachers and his parents were extremely happy for his success.

He jumped out of happiness and said aloud,

"God helps those who help themselves".

* * * * *

MY LEARNING

This has been a good learning experience for me ever since my childhood. Whenever I complain about something to God, for not getting it, I immediately see whether I really worked towards it properly or not. This keeps me grounded and more focussed towards my desired goal. After achieving the goal, I always thank the Almighty for blessing me for the right kind of potential to work towards it. As it is always said, 'God helps those who help themselves.'

MORAL

God helps those who help themselves

2.

Sow good and good things happen... for real

One day, my cousin Sheela, who was ten years old, finished her home-work and started watching ' Tom and Jerry ' on T.V.

Suddenly, she heard someone screaming. Though the voice was coming from a distance, it was loud enough to make out that someone was screaming loudly out of pain. She immediately went to the window and peeped out to see what was going on.

"Please do not beat me aaaaa !!!!!, please do not kick me aauuch!!!!!"

Sheela saw a young rich man abusing and kicking an old lame man on the road side. She felt very bad about it.Before she could go down with her mother to help him, she saw her neighbor uncle talking to that young rich man.

Her uncle was having an argument with that person and after sometime that young man left in aggression and the neighbour helped the lame man by taking him to the nearby doctor immediately. The old man was hurt badly.

Sheela was upset with what she saw and asked her mother, " Mumma wasn't that man a bad person?"

My mother said, "Yes, my child, he was indeed a bad man, we should never hurt someone who is not as strong and powerful as we are. Instead, we should always help others and seek their blessings. Blessings always help us in our difficult times. Helping others is a sign of being a good human."

Sheela patiently heard everything that her mother told. Her mother always taught her good things. She trusted her mother even if she did not understand anything at that particular time. This time Sheela wondered what her mother meant by difficult times as she was too small to understand that.

Sheela always remembered her mother's kind words. Few days later, when Sheela was coming back from school with one of her friends and her mother in the afternoon, she saw an old lady sitting near her house who was sobbing. It was a hot afternoon. Before entering her home, she went close to that lady and enquired the reason of her sadness.

Sheela was initially a little scared but still gathered the courage of doing what she wanted to do. Sheela asked her the reason of her sorrow.

The old lady replied sobbing, "I have not had food in the last three days and I am very thirsty too." Listening to this, Sheela went running inside her house, she kept her bag properly, removed her shoes and went running inside the kitchen.

Her mother used to leave her lunch covered with a plate before leaving for her office. She picked up her plate and went outside to give food to the old lady. She also took a glass of water for her.

Sheela said, "Please drink water and eat the food."

The old lady grabbed the glass of water, drank it and ate the food in a haste. Sheela could see the happiness on the old lady's face. The old lady was actually hungry.

After emptying the plate, the lady said, "Thank you my child and God bless you." The lady blessed Sheela for her kindness and left. Sheela was also very happy to help her. She actually implemented what she was taught at home.

She happily ate few cookies instead of her lunch.

She narrated the whole story to her mother when she came home in the evening.

Her mother was happy to know that Sheela was learning to do good deeds on her own. She appreciated her and gave her a hug.

Few weeks later one evening, Sheela was playing with her friends in a nearby garden. Her parents were back from their office and were having tea.

There was some construction work going on near that garden. Since there was a slope in that garden, a big wooden log came rolling on the ground and hit Sheela hard on her leg.

Sheela screamed out of pain, "O Mumma, help me… O God help me, my leg, its paining." She tried a lot to get up and walk on her own but was unable to do so.

One of her friends ran to call her parents. They came running to the garden. Her friends were sure that she must have fractured her leg. The contractor from the construction site also came to apologize on behalf of the laborer.

Since she was in pain, her parents did not say anything to the contractor but just warned him to be careful next time and asked him to pray for their daughter. She was in acute pain. She was also scared of getting aplaster on her leg. Her parents immediately took her to the nearby hospital.

The doctor examined her properly and asked them to get an X-Ray done immediately.

After looking at the X-Ray, the doctor said, "Please do not worry. It is not a fracture. It is just a sprain which will take few days to cure." He further said that Sheela would be able to walk properly after few days.

He prescribed some tablets, ointment and asked her to rest her leg for the coming few days. Sheela and her parents were little relaxed and came back home.

Though in pain, that night Sheela was lying down on her bed and resting, she immediately remembered the old lady's blessings and her mother's kind words. Sheela called her mother and said, 'Thank you Mumma for teaching me good things and now I understand the meaning of difficult time.' She also thanked that old lady in her prayers for blessing her and also recollected how she shared her food with her that afternoon. She never thought that such a small deed of kindness would help her in this way. This thought brought a smile on Sheela's face. She slept in peace after sometime.

* * * * *

MY LEARNING

This incident in my cousin's life taught me to always be good to others and seek their blessings. We are born humans but we have to learn to be human. We must learn our lessons well and contribute kindness and goodness in others' lives too. I learnt to build a chain of exchanging goodness and allow it to become the key to our happiness.

MORAL

Be human – Be happy

3.

BEING CALM AND POLITE ....
A GAME CHANGER

Natasha was one year senior to me in school. She was very good in academics, sports and extra – curricular activities. These reasons were sufficient for her to have more enemies and less friends in class. She was a very well-mannered and a kind hearted girl. She was good to everyone and did not bother what the others thought of her. Most of her classmates were jealous of her.

Shipra her classmate said, "Natasha always acts to be polite and be in good books of the teachers."

Natasha knew about the ill talks but would always say, "all are my friends and they are good."

Whenever someone misbehaved in class the teacherwould always say, "learn to behave properly and be like Natasha." The girls would murmur in the class and say, "Our teacher does not like us, only because of Natasha."

It was winter season and the school planned a one-day picnic for the students. Everyone was excited to have one leisure day with their school friends. Natasha too was super excited.

Finally, the day of picnic came. Natasha carried too many eatables and outdoor games with her. She wanted to share her things and enjoy the day to the fullest.

Everyone seemed to be super excited on the day of picnic. All of them came to school on time and stepped in the bus that took them to the picnic spot.

Every student along-with their respective teachers were singing songs in the bus and munching snacks. They happily reached the spot and after listening to the instructions by their teachers, started playing in groups and doing whatever they liked. Few started eating and others started exploring the place.

Suddenly, Natasha heard someone shouting, "you are lying, you are a cheat." She turned around and saw a group of her classmates fighting with a shopkeeper.

When she went near, one of the girls pushed her back saying, "You stay out of this, we can handle it ourselves." Natasha did not feel bad and waited for some time.

The quarrel continued.

Instead, it heated up even more. She saw the shopkeeper arguing with her classmates.

Before the voice could reach the teachers, Natasha tried to intervene one more time to know the reason. This time one of the girls said, "We bought some goodies from the shopkeeper and gave him a Rs.100/- note. He is denying and not returning our balance money. He is simply saying that we did not give him money."

Exchange of foul words continued. One girl called him a liar and the other called him a cheater. One girl said, "My mother will scold me for losing the money" and so on. The shopkeeper was also angry with the girls and said, "Why will I return you something that I have not taken?" He further said, "Is this the way you are taught in school to behave with others?"

Natasha thought for a while. She knew that her friends were not lying. She went near the shopkeeper and said, "Sir, will you please listen to me and be quite for some time." She also whispered to her friends, "You will get your money back, please maintain silence for some time. Let me try once."

This time everyone agreed to what Natasha was saying as she assured them to get their money back. Moreover, everyone was tired of repeating the same argument.

She went towards the shopkeeper and said softly, "Uncle, please drink a glass of water and sit down for some time. We can talk about this a little later." She offered him water. He drank the water and sat down on his chair.

She further said, "Now tell me uncle, what happened."

Listening to her polite, humble and respectful voice, the shopkeeper calmed down and started explaining the situation to her.

He said, "Few girls came to my shop and started asking for ice-cream, chocolate and soft drink. I started removing the things from the refrigerator. Two of them gave me Rs.100/- note but the third one did not give me any money. Before I could return the other two girls' money, the third one started abusing me for not returning her balance amount. I told her that she never gave me a Rs. 100/- note."

After listening to the shopkeeper, she said, "I request you kindly check your cash box one more time, you might have missed on the note." She also assured the shopkeeper saying, "If you do not find the note in your cash box, I will request all my friends to check their bags again." With her soft words, she also said, "You will surely find the note as my friends will never lie. They all are good girls, please do not worry." Listening to these lines of Natasha, her friends started liking and trusting her. They felt ashamed of their behavior towards her.

The shopkeeper agreed to what she said. As soon as he looked down towards the cash box, he saw a folded Rs.100/- note lying down on floor. He happily spoke aloud, "I found the note." He further apologized and said, "I did not see the note lying on the floor as all the girls started abusing me and I lost my temper." He thanked Natasha for listening to him patiently and finding a solution.

Natasha approached her friends and said, "My friends please take your balance money back." The girls felt ashamed of themselves. One of them said, "we promise you that we will always be polite to others." The other one said, "We are sorry for our attitude towards you." One of them spoke aloud, "We always misunderstood you."

All of them said, "Please forgive us and be our friend." Natasha smiled and hugged all her friends. One of her friends also said, "Today we have learnt how to handle a complex situation with ease by just being polite and thoughtful and we can always find a good solution to various situations with a calm mind and polite behavior."

Natasha requested her friends to apologize for their behavior towards the shopkeeper. All of them unitedly went to the shopkeeper and apologized.

This day was one of the happiest days of her life. After this incident everyone became Natasha's friend and tried to implement her kind of goodness wherever and whenever possible in their day-to-day life.

MY LEARNING

All this happened in front of my eyes. I still remember Natasha and learnt a lesson for my lifetime. I learnt to be polite and calm while handling complex situations with ease. I also learnt at a very tender age that, heated arguments mess up a situation and increase our problems. Whereas, polite discussions lead to happy solutions.

MORAL

Politeness helps overcome difficult situations

4.

AN EXPERIENCE CAN CHANGE YOUR LIFE … FOR BETTER

Amar, my classmate in fourth standard was a very good athlete. He always used to stand first in every running race. He was not only good in academics and sports but in his behaviour too. Everyone used to appreciate his dedication towards sports. He used to win the competitions at interschool level, district level and also state level.

Our sports coach appreciated him and said, "Keep up the hard work and you will soon become a national champion."

Amar was very particular and ate healthy food, made it a point to study regularly, put in his hours of practice as an athlete. To top it all, he never missed saying his prayers.At the same time there were few very bad habits in Amar which he refused to accept and rectify. He used to politely give justifications for them.

He had a very bad habit of spilling his food while eating, he used to waste food and would always keep his dress and surroundings dirty. His friends often told him to avoid spilling and wasting food.

Whenever the sweeper came to clean the classroom, he would find spilt food around Amar's seat. The sweeper would easily make out where Amar ate his lunch. The sweeper complained about this to the class teacher. Since Amar was a good student, she explained him the importance of food and asked him not to repeat it again. Amar nodded his head in front of the class teacher but continued to spill his food. This had become his habit.

At home, his house maid would clean everything and wash his clothes, so his mother was not aware of his habit. Whenever they used to go out with family, his parents would tell him not to do such things and at times ignored as they thought he would learn as he grows.

When the coach observed these things, he said, "Amar you are a good athlete and have great potential to improve but, you will have to leave these bad habits."

He too used to explain the importance of cleanliness to Amar. One day the coach said the same thing to him. He said," you have to keep everything neat and tidy as, Cleanliness is next to Godliness."

But, Amar ignored this by justifying that, God has blessed him with good food, good sports qualities and academic excellence so these things do not matter much.

He continued to do the same until finally the time came when he learnt the lesson of 'Cleanliness'.

Amar was selected for a fifteen days intense training sports camp. He was very happy and excited for the camp. He thought that he would get proper training to participate at the National level competitions. He packed his bags and went for the camp.

Everyone was given an individual room. The room was to be

cleaned by the players themselves. But Amar knew nothing about this as, he only used to focus on his practice and all the other things were taken care of by others. The dirt just kept piling up day by day.

He was learning all the new techniques taught to him very nicely and he was doing pretty good. He was being highly appreciated by his new coaches too. He was very happy.

Suddenly one day, after a week-long training, he fell sick. He suffered from stomach ache, vomiting and mild fever. The coach immediately called the doctor.

As soon as the doctor stepped inside the room, he took his foot back saying, "I will not enter this room I have never seen such a dirty, filthy and stinking room ever in my life !!!"

"How can a sportsperson have such a dirty room. A person can never stay healthy in such unhealthy surrounding." The doctor actually started complaining and blaming the coach for not bothering about his students' personal cleanliness and hygiene.

Amar felt very insulted and ashamed of himself. For the first time he realized his mistake and felt very bad as one of his favorite coaches was being insulted by the doctor.

Though Amar was feeling very weak, he gathered strength to get up and say sorry to the doctor.

He said, "Doctor, I am very sorry for this, I have invited my own illness by not taking care of my surroundings."

He further said, "I took everything for granted, but now I promise that I will always keep my surroundings neat and clean and maintain hygiene and above all never waste my food. God is everywhere so along with my prayers I should keep everything clean, only then God will be near me."

He also apologized in front of his coach, "Sir, I am really sorry for not listening to your advice."

Amar was sick throughout the training camp and lost the opportunity to participate in the national championship this time.

This training camp proved to be a learning experience and Amar learnt his lesson well. After coming back from the camp, he apologized to his parents, housemaid, teachers, friends, his coach and also the sweepers in school. He appreciated their concern for rectifying him but regretted for not listening to them. He promised everyone to follow good habits from now onwards.

He started taking that extra effort for his own personal hygiene and cleanliness of his surroundings along with his daily routine. He started taking care of all his things that he used to ignore earlier.

Amar learnt a lesson of his life during the camp. He was a changed person now and was happy with this change. Next year, Amar got another opportunity to participate in the camp.

MY LEARNING

From Amar's experience I too, learnt

"Cleanliness is next to Godliness"

Though I always used to believe in it, I saw everything happening in front of me which left an impact on my mind.

I have learnt a lot from others experience and try to inculcate that quality in myself. Cleanliness not only gives us a lot of positivity but also helps us stay healthy.

MORAL

Cleanliness is next to Godliness

5.

A Bitter Experience …
A Sweet Lesson

My neighbor Geeta was a good girl. She was twelve years of age. We used to play together almost every evening. She was good at studies and used to help me with my studies whenever I asked for help.

As it is commonly said that no one is perfect, Geeta too had some good qualities and had one habit of leaving food in her plate. She used to fill her plate with excess food and later on leave it. Her mother often guided her to take small servings and take another one when needed, but Geeta never obeyed. Geeta always used to say, "I will finish the food Maa, I am very hungry." But, would leave the food as always.

Her mother would say, "Geeta please finish your food. You should respect food that God has given you." Geeta would nod her head and say, "Yes Mumma, I will never leave my food next time," and the next time would never come. She used to forget what she said and do the same mistake time and again.

She not only wasted her food at home but also her friends' food in school. She would ask for some food from her friends' tiffin and later on leave it. Never did she realize that her friends were left hungry. Her friends gradually stopped sharing food with her. Her mother was very upset with her daughter's behavior.

One day she said angrily, "One day God will teach you that disrespecting food is disrespecting God."

Days passed by and one day the school announced a school picnic.

Geeta was over-excited about the picnic. Everyday she discussed what all would they do that day and felt happy. A day prior to the picnic day, she went to the market in the evening with her parents to buy her favorite snacks, muffins, chocolates and fruits. That day all of them had dinner in a nearby restaurant. After coming back home, Geeta slept a little early as she had to wake up a little early the next morning. She forgot to keep the snacks and other stuff in her bag.

Next morning, she woke up happily with the morning alarm. She quickly brushed her teeth and went to have her bath. That particular day, though her mother had to go to the office little early, she managed to make Geeta's favorite sandwiches. While leaving for work, Geeta's mother knocked the bathroom door and reminded Geeta to keep everything in her picnic bag. She replied, "Don't worry Mumma, I will do it." Her mother left for her office. Geeta got ready properly. Out of excitement she forgot to keep all the eatables in her bag. She did not even have her breakfast before leaving home that day. She quickly picked up her bag and left for school.

After reaching school she met all her friends and started discussing about the day ahead. They all were very happy. All of them were singing songs and chit chatting on their way to the picnic spot. Finally, they reached the picnic spot which was quite far from the school. It was indeed a very beautiful place with different types of play areas. All started playing. They were having a good time.

After sometime everyone started eating food. They all were hungry and tired after playing. Geeta was still playing. Her friend Priya called her, "Geeta come, let us eat first and play later." But Geeta said, "I will eat later, I want to play more." All her friends were busy enjoying their food.

After sometime, Geeta too got tired of playing and felt very hungry. By that time all her friends had already finished their food and had started playing again. She went close to her bag and excitedly opened it to enjoy her favorite snacks. As soon as she opened her bag, she realized that she had forgotten to put the eatables in her bag!

She was really upset to see only a water bottle, cap and a napkin inside the bag.

She was extremely hungry by now and did not know what to do. She drank water and sat there for a while.

She could not ask for food from any of her friends as they had stopped sharing food with her. She somehow gathered courage and approached her best friend, Priya. Priya was on a swing at that time.

Geeta shyly asked, "Priya can I share your food."

Priya said, "Sorry Geeta, I have already finished my tiffin and just have water with me." Geeta could not even tell Priya that she had not eaten anything since morning. She was into tears but somehow tried to hide them.

Geeta was left with only one option to drink water and stay hungry.

Her mother's words echoed in her ears, "One day God will teach you that disrespecting food is disrespecting God."

She now realized that God had punished her for wasting her food all the time. She learnt the lesson of respecting food at all times. She decided not to waste the precious food ever after. She prayed to God to forgive her for her mistake.

After she came back home, she entered the kitchen to grab some cookies. While eating, she was into tears. When her mother came back home, Geeta promised her mother that she will always finish her food and never waste it. Geeta also apologized for ignoring her mother's wise advice. She then shared her day's experience with her mother.

Her mother felt bad that her daughter had been hungry through the day but, was also happy that her little girl started respecting food. Geeta's mother served freshly made dinner to her, hugged her and helped her to sleep well.

Geeta narrated this incident to me when we were playing in the garden the next evening. She was really feeling bad for not having anything to eat on the picnic day but was also happy for knowing the importance of food which she used to waste all the time. Geeta once again said sorry to the Almighty and also thanked Him for making her learn this good habit of respecting food.

MY LEARNING

I too realized how every bite of food is important and a gift of God to us. The food that is served in our plate is just the finished product. It is grown in the field, processed somewhere else, passes through a long journey from the wholesaler to the retailer and then bought by us. Our parents work hard, earn money and buy groceries with that money. It is further cooked with love and then served in our plate. I always used to finish the food that I was served on my plate. But, from that day onwards I started taking food in small portions and finished every bit of it. I always prayed before having my meal and thanked the Almighty. With this ritual, I have always had stomach full of food. Thank you, God.

MORAL

Respect food (and it will respect you)

6.

SELF REALIZATION…
THE BEST REALISATION

Arjun my cousin, was a very naughty child. Though he was in his early teens, he was always very rude and never ever had respect or gratitude towards anyone. I used to meet him only during my summer vacation. We, as a family, used to go to my maternal uncle's home to spend few days of my holidays.

One afternoon, an elderly person was sleeping peacefully on the roadside. Arjun thought of doing something mischievous. He went there and pinched him hard. The old man suddenly screamed out of pain. Arjun laughed and said, "Hahaha!!!!, I enjoyed pinching you, your skin is very soft." Arjun did not even realize that the elderly person was in pain. Arjun found happiness and peace when he troubled others. My uncle and aunt were really upset with his behavior.

They would keep saying, "Arjun please behave properly." "Arjun please be respectful."

"Arjun, please be helpful to others."

He would never listen to them and keep doing the same. Gradually, he turned to be a very rude boy.

His parents used to pray to God, "O God please help our child to understand humanity."

One fine day, their true prayers were heard.

Arjun was very fond of eating Chinese food. One day he went to his favorite Chinese restaurant with his parents. Chinese food was rarely available in restaurants in those days. His parents ordered his favorite 'Hakka Noodles' and 'Manchurian' for him. Arjun was super excited and very hungry too. He harshly ordered the waiter, "Bring it really fast, I am very hungry."

In the mean while Arjun's attention was drawn towards the music that was on. Arjun got so excited that he started dancing and jumping on the chair. His father said, "Sit down Arjun, do not jump, you will fall down." But he would not stop.

Arjun's mother said, "Sit down and relax, food will come any moment." He did not listen to anyone of them. Coincidently, his swinging arm hit the waiter who was bringing their food. Arjun hit the waiter so hard that the tray fell down from the waiter's hands.

Instead of being apologetic, Arjun got angry with the waiter as his favorite dishes were all around the floor!

He immediately started abusing the waiter assuming it was his mistake. He said, "O waiter you do not know how to do your work properly, you have spoilt my food." He also said, "You are just a waiter and will remain a waiter because of your inefficiency. You have also spoilt my new clothes. You will have to pay our bill." He spoke whatever came in his mind to insult the waiter. The waiter was standing silently and observing the ill- mannered boy. His

Juvenile Parables

parents were really ashamed of Arjun's behavior and asked him to say sorry to the waiter as he is elder to him and above all it was Arjun's mistake. But, Arjun refused to apologize.

When Arjun stopped abusing, the waiter went inside and served the dishes again. He served them well with a smiling face.

After they finished the food, the waiter apologized for his mistake and looking at Arjun, he politely said, "My child, I am the owner of your favorite restaurant. I started working here as a waiter and now I own my own chain of restaurants which is your favorite." Arjun was shocked to listen to his kind words. The waiter further said, "One of my boys is unwell today, so I am doing his duty. According to me no work is big or small. Work is work and we should have dignity of labor. We should respect every work and do it dedicatedly. That is the key to prosperity."

These kind and wise words of the owner said it all. Arjun was shocked and realized his mistake. He stood up and said, "Sorry uncle, I misbehaved with you, I will never do it again and will behave properly. My parents have tried their level best to inculcate good habits in me but, I was the one who never took them seriously. It was my mistake for always taking them for granted." He apologized to his parents for his ill and rude behavior.

From that day onwards Arjun's behavior changed. He had never met a person like him before. He then realized that he was unknowingly or ignorantly taking everything for granted in life never realizing that everything needs so much of effort and sincerity. He learnt his lesson well. He also went to all the people one by one to whomsoever he had been rude ever and apologized for his behavior.

When I went to my maternal uncle's place during my vacation, I saw a different Arjun altogether. I went near him and hesitantly asked, "How did you change so much my dear brother?" It was then that Arjun narrated the entire transforming incident to me.

Seeing the changed Arjun, I was really astonished. I was feeling happy for him and my uncle and aunt too.

MY LEARNING

From that day onwards I started respecting everyone and everyone's work. I started respecting the people as they are and was never disrespectful to anyone. As everyone has their own priorities and preferences in life, we just have to let them be and never make fun of anyone's situation or condition.

I am thankful to God for conveying these values in such a wonderful manner in my life.

MORAL

Have Dignity of Labour.

7.

THOUGH SMALL ....
THERE IS A LOT WE CAN DO

Sunil was a ten years old boy who lived in a small chawl near our home. We used to play together in the evenings. He lived happily with his parents. He was their only child. His father was a vegetable vendor and mother was a home maker. At times, his mother would go to their vegetable shop to help her husband. They all lived in that small house. His parents wanted him to study well and become successful in life. Both of them also taught him good things so that he grows up to be a good human being. He learnt them well and implemented the same in his day-to-day life. He was good in his studies and was loved by his teachers too. He used to focus well in his studies and get good marks.

They were all leading a happy life until one day his father fell sick. He suffered from very high fever for almost a month. He was bed ridden. He was growing weaker and weaker by each passing day and the cause of his illness was not being diagnosed. He grew so weak that he was unable to do anything on his own. His vegetable shop got shut down as he was unable to go to buy the vegetables from the wholesale market. They were left with very little money. His parents were stressed about their near future and also the future of their beloved son. Since they did not have much money, the local doctor could not ask him to go for expensive check-ups. The doctor kept on giving him medicines to help him gain his strength back.

For this reason, the mother started working as a house-maid in few houses to earn their living. Along with her work, she also took proper care of her husband.

Sunil did not realize that his father was not earning anything anymore. His parents would never disturb him in his daily life routine. Both of them suffered that difficult time by themselves. They both just wanted Sunil to focus on becoming a learned man when he grows up.

His mother was left alone to do all the household chores, take care of his father and also earn money for livelihood.

Sunil was kept away from the reality. He just used to ask his father that when will you be fine? His father used to reply positively by saying, "Very soon my son, you focus on your studies."

One day while coming back from school, Sunil saw his mother mopping the floor in a nearby house.

He was surprised to see his mother working in someone else's house. She also looked very tired while working.

When his mother came back home, he asked, "Maa you look very tired and why were you mopping the floor of that house?" His mother was a person who would never complain about anything. She simply said, "I am just working in their house as a maid servant." Sunil came near his mother to hug her. As soon as he hugged her, he realized that she had high fever. He said, "Maa you have high fever. Please sit down." He helped her to sit down and brought her a glass of water.

She thanked Sunil for his gesture and after sometime got up to cook something. Sunil said, "Please let me know what to do Maa." His mother said, "Do not worry my son, I will manage." Then Sunil said, "I wish to help you. I do not know what to do as you have never asked me to do anything other than my own work. I wish to learn to do household things from today onwards." That day both of them managed to cook. All of them had food together and later on Sunil gave medicine to his father and mother.

His parents went off to sleep but Sunil was still awake. Now was the time when Sunil realized that his mother was getting too tired of doing everything, all by herself. His father was also unwell. Though he could not realize entirely what his parents were going through, he thought that he was spending so much time playing, studying and going to school and there is no one to help and take care of his parents. He finally decided to finish his work quickly and help his parents. Next day morning he went to his parents and said, "I am a big and strong boy, please tell me, how can I help you both."

His parents were overwhelmed to hear these lines from their little child. Both had tears in their eyes. They said, "We are very happy with your kind gesture towards us. God Bless you." They asked him to do whatever he could do without compromising with his studies.

From that day onwards Sunil used to get up a little early and help his father to have a bath and dress up. He also helped his mother

Juvenile Parables

in cleaning the house. Since his mother would not allow him to go near the stove, he would do everything other than cooking. He slowly learnt to cut vegetables and wash the dishes. After coming back from school, he would take a little rest and help his mother in washing the utensils, clothes and even go to the market to buy things.

Along with all these things he used to say his prayers, finish his homework and also played for some time with his friends. He reduced his play time and finished his studies quickly. His efficiency level and speed gradually improved.

Soon, his father too started feeling better and regained his health. He could now perform his personal routine all by himself. His mother did not feel tired anymore and recovered well. After a couple of months, his father started going to work again. Sunil was very happy that he had now learnt to contribute towards his family. He was happier than before and so were his parents. Sunil continued helping his parents. He became more responsible. His life became a lesson for all his friends. He lived happily with his family.

MY LEARNING

He does not even know that I learnt so much from his behavior. Whenever I saw him, I would always learn different ways of helping elders and being happy. Improving our efficiency level by every changing phase, accepting life as it comes started becoming a habit which ultimately improved my thought process. I became more conscious about our elders' contribution in our lives which ultimately helped me to be a good human being.

MORAL

Always assist your family.

8.

BEATREND-SETTER

Vijay, my neighbor was a very exceptional child at the age of twelve. He was very good at studies, he prayed every day, ate his food by himself, did not waste anything, always kept everything in order. He was very good at sports and also in extra-curricular activities. He became an independent boy at very young age. He was respectful, disciplined and obedient. There was so much to learn from him. Everyone was fond of Vijay.

The quality that made him different from other children was that he used to go to a nearby old age home to serve the elders and give them few moments of happiness. His friends used to watch T.V. when free, but he preferred going to that old age home. He used to watch T.V. only to improve his knowledge and not to pass his time. He enjoyed being with the elderly people. He was well brought up.

In school, Vijay's classmate Ravi was a very naughty boy.

Though he was new to the school, he used to trouble his classmates all the time. He used to snatch their pencils when they were writing or even scribble in their note books. Whenever someone went to the class-teacher to complain, she used to say that Ravi is new to all of us, please give him time, he will change. Help him in all possible ways so that he starts being good to you all. Ravi used to observe Vijay all the time and wanted to be like him.

After a few days he went to talk to him. He said, "My friend, I want to be like you." Vijay just looked at him and smiled. He said, "You are already like me." Ravi said, "I wish to be as happy and relaxed as you are. You never get annoyed with anyone complain about anyone. You are not like others."

Days passed and Ravi kept on observing Vijay. He wanted to be as happy as Ravi but ended up troubling him. Vijay just used to be sweet to him and ask him to be kind to others and be friends to them. Ravi would listen to him but ended up doing the same mischief again and again. He gradually started losing friends and was left alone. Everyone gave up on him and stopped even talking to him.

Ravi got even more irritated and troubled everyone.

He was always unhappy despite of doing what he liked (troubling others). The one and only classmate that was still talking to him was Vijay, though he was troubling him too. Ravi always used to see the same happy, calm and relaxed Vijay. He started troubling Vijay more and more just to attract his attention, but Vijay remained his old good self.

Inside his heart, Ravi idealised Vijay. One day, he gave up on troubling Vijay and went to talk to him once again. He said, "My friend, I want to be like you." Vijay just looked at him and smiled. Heagain replied , "You are already like me." Ravi said, "I wish to be as happy as you are. You never get annoyed with me or anyone

Juvenile Parables

else. I wish to know the reason of your happiness. How can I be like you?" Vijay simply said, "You are already like me. Just seek more and more blessings." Ravi got surprised. "Blessings?" Vijay nodded his head. From that day onwards Ravi started being with Vijay. Gradually, both of them became fond of each other.

One day, Ravi asked Vijay, "Though I wish to be like you but am unable to understand how." Vijay politely said, "Please do not be like me, be yourself. Just think before doing anything." Ravi further asked him, "How do you remain so happy all the time. I always envy you." Vijay smiled and said, "My dear friend, I cannot tell you how, but it gives me immense happiness when I do good to others.

Little smile on that persons' face fills my day with immense happiness." By just being with Vijay, Ravi started transforming. He started being friends with others and started helping others in little ways. He gradually started being happy from within. Everybody could see the change in Ravi. As Vijay used to go to the old age home regularly, Ravi asked him the reason for going there. He said, "It gives me happiness to be there but, you have to experience it by yourself."

"My parents have always taught me to gather blessings, as blessings give strength when we are in any hardship in life."

Ravi asked, "have you ever felt like that?" Vijay said, "Yes, I always feel that I am being helped in every small or big situation. I feel this very strongly within myself. This is also the reason why I remain happy all the time."

Ravi was touched by the kind words of Vijay. He said, "My friend, no matter how difficult your deeds seem to me right now, I will always try to be like you one day." He also said, " I have always been very naughty and have troubled everyone, but have never felt that inner happiness as you said in your words."

Few days later, Ravi accompanied him to the old age home. When he entered that place, he saw really old people who started smiling and blessing Vijay as soon as they saw him. Vijay helped them in whichever way they wanted. Everyone waited for him every day as a ray of happy hope. Vijay also played games with a few. Ravi just observed everything.

That day while coming back home, Ravi said, "I have never felt as happy as today. I actually cannot express myself to you. I am elated. I am falling short of words to express my happiness. I am speechless. The only thing that I can say now is that there is immense happiness and gratitude within me."

He also said, "I will accompany you, whenever you are coming here. I feel I met my grandparents. They were so nice and loving. I used to love being with them. Both died in an accident few years back."

He further said, "Now I know why you said that you have to feel it by yourself." He further thanked Vijay for introducing him to this place.

Vijay was even happier that Ravi would accompany him. Then, both of them could do good things for elders. Soon both of them started sharing the same thought process.

I was very small at that time, but learnt good things from him. At times I went to that old age home with my parents and met everyone. I still feel that warmth whenever I think of that place and even the kind of boy Vijay was who, could change a naughty boy like Ravi into such a kind person and broaden the path to eternal happiness.

MORAL

Serve the elders and gain blessings for a lifetime.

9.

SHARING WITH OTHERS IS CARING FOR ONESELF

A boy named Rahul lived near my home. He was from a well-off family. We used to play together almost every evening. He was very selfish and arrogant. He would never share his things with anyone. Whenever we used to ask for his ball to play, he would always say, "No, I will not let anyone play with my ball, it is too expensive." He would play with our things and kept saying that they were of such cheap quality.

As time passed, he became violent and aggressive with his friends. Gradually, because of this, he started losing his friends one by one. No one wanted to play with him. This made him angry.

Rahul's best friend was Mohan. He was from a well-off family too. Both of them used to go to school together. Mohan was just the opposite of Rahul. Mohan always wanted Rahul to become a good boy and Rahul always asked Mohan to become like him. Rahul would often tell Mohan, "Do not share your things with others, they will spoil them, play with their things and enjoy." Mohan always replied, "You should once feel the joy of sharing and giving, it will give you immense happiness."

One day while walking to school they saw two poor children starving. Both begged for food in front of them. Mohan immediately stopped and opened his tiffin and give them his food. Rahul held Mohan's hand and said, "Why did you give them your food? You will have to starve the whole day." Mohan politely said, "It gives me happiness if I share what God has given me and above all both of them were more needy than I am. I had stomach full breakfast before leaving for school. I will be fine till evening, do not worry."

Mohan suggested Rahul to try sharing his things atleast once, to feel happy. He also reminded him of a saying, 'Sharing is Caring.'

As always, Rahul did not pay much attention to what his friend said but, thought of giving it a try. He thought, if he did anything like this, the other children would make fun of him.

Days passed and he was busy with the same behavior pattern and became more and more restless by each passing day.

As suggested by his friend Mohan, he wanted to try the suggested gesture but did not know when to try it.

One fine day Rahul was going to the school all alone as Mohan was unwell that day. An old man was sitting by the road side begging for food. Rahul looked here and there to confirm if no one was looking at him. There was nobody on the road at that time.

Rahul thought of sharing some food with that person.

He secretly opened his lunch box and said, "Baba please take this food." The old man thanked him and said, "God bless you, my child." Rahul felt very happy and ran from there before anyone could see him.

After running for some time, he lowered his speed. As soon as he started walking slowly, he observed a blind man standing by the road side and waiting for someone to help him cross the road. Rahul thought of doing this deed of kindness again but his heart beat was still moving very fast. He was doing something absolutely opposite to his nature. He gradually gathered courage and asked that man, "Uncle, may I help you cross the road?" The man smilingly nodded his head. After crossing the road, the man said, "Thank you and God bless you my child." Rahul was almost into tears as he had never heard such kind words for himself from anyone.

That whole day Rahul was very emotional but happy. He smiled at whoever crossed by him and did not get angry with anyone. His inner happiness was over-powering him as he was overwhelmed by his own changed behavior.

He was quiet the whole day as he was continuously thinking about the new feelings within him. He was confused with the change within him.

The children were surprised to see his behavior but remained away from him that day. They thought that he might be up to some new mischief. Days passed and Rahul started doing something kind everyday but secretly. He started being less abusive and less aggressive to his friends.

After few days when Mohan joined him back to school, he saw the changed Rahul. After a couple of days, he told Rahul, "I am very happy to see the positive change in you, as you seem to be happier than ever before. What is the secret of your happiness?" Rahul honestly thanked Mohan for suggesting him to be kind to others and share his things with others. He said, "I have really started feeling happy and don't feel like fighting with anyone anymore. Thank you once again and please be by my side to guide me wherever I go wrong."

Both of them hugged each other and promised to remain best friends. Slowly he started sharing his things with all of us while playing during evenings. He got back his lost friends. In school, one of the boys came near him and said, "It is my birthday today and I want to give you two chocolates." Rahul was elated.

These small deeds started changing Rahul from within. Gradually, his behavior changed and it gave him immense happiness.

Mohan was very happy to see his friend changing for the better. Rahul finally came to Mohan one day and thanked him again in front of all of us, "Now I am experiencing the joy of giving and am thankful to you for constantly making me aware of it. I give all the credit to you for changing me." He further said, "I apologize for my misbehavior with you all while playing." He also told everyone how he secretly started sharing what God had given him. Everyone was very happy for Rahul and all of us became his friends once again.

MY LEARNING

As I started playing with Rahul again, I also learnt the good gestures taught by Mohan. I started doing the small deeds of kindness by sharing and giving my things to others more frequently. This in turn helped me to have that feeling of fullness, gratitude and happiness for what I have.

MORAL

Feel the joy of giving and sharing.

10.

YOUR HEALTH IS IN YOUR HANDS

Rompo was a plump eleven-year-old boy. He was my best friend's cousin. His parents were a working couple. They both had to leave early in the morning to reach their work place. Rompo had a maid to look after him during the day.

He loved eating potato chips and watching television. After coming back from school, he used to throw his bag and sit to watch T.V. and have his food. After that he would surely have a packet of chips and sit down to watch his favorite channel and then sleep on the sofa itself. He was too fond of junk food. He was a foody. In the evening, after getting up from his sleep he used to ask his maid to bring pakodas or samosas for him. If the maid would suggest him to have milk and some healthy snacks, he would always say that he would have milk at night, before sleeping and eat food when his parents were back home and would again start watching T.V.

If the maid asked him to go to the garden and play with his friends, he would always say that he would go after watching his favorite programme on T.V. The maid would go to get his favorite snack and then get busy in cooking dinner for the family.

After eating the junk food and watching television for quite some time, he would get up to finish his school home work. His parents would return when his homework was about to finish. The maid used to leave after his parents came back home. He would happily welcome his parents and then spend time with them.

After having family dinner, he would again watch T.V. for some more time and sleep. This became his daily routine.

Rompo was gaining weight day by day.

His mother was worried about his eating habits and immobility. Whenever she used to say, "Rompo you must go out and play with your friends every day in the evening." He would reply, "Yes Mumma I wish to go but by the time my favourite programme gets over all my friends are already back home. I try to complete my homework before you both are back home." His mother did not know what to say. She worried about him but could not find a solution.

He would never do any exercise, and in school would always make excuses in the sports period.

As it is wisely said – 'Excess of everything is bad.' Rompo became more and more obese.It became difficult for him to even go to school regularly and the students started teasing him, "Aye fatty sit at home, don't come to school." Others said, "You need two benches to sit in class." He felt bad for some time but forgot about it once back home and followed the same routine of eating and watching T.V. Actually, watching television would take him away from the real life to the imaginary life.

He liked studying and scored good marks in his exams. Due to his immobility and wrong eating habits, his health started deteriorating. He used to get breathless after walking for some time. He was obese from outside and unhealthy and weak from inside. He started developing serious health issues wherein it became difficult for him to even do his routine work. It became difficult for him to move. But still he would not do what his parents asked him to do.

One Sunday evening their television got spoilt. He told his father to call a mechanic and get it fixed soon as his favourite programme would begin in another hour. His father immediately refused to get it repaired and asked him to move out of the house and play with his friends. He said, "Please call the mechanic first and then I will go out for some time." His father strictly refused, "I will not get the T.V. repaired until you go to play."

Rompo got angry with his father and tried to rush from the living room to his bedroom. When he turned angrily to go aside, glass plate fell from the table when his hand hit the table and he accidently hurt himself with broken pieces of glass.

Suddenly, there was blood flowing from his right foot. He got scared and could not even help himself to get up as his foot was paining. He screamed out of pain. As soon as his father saw this, he immediately called the family doctor. It was actually difficult for his father to lift him from the ground single handedly. Both his parents somehow lifted him from the ground and made him sit on the sofa and gave him first aid before the doctor came. Rompo could not even go to the clinic to get his dressing done.

Rompo thought that he is left with no friend, does not have T.V. to watch, is unable to go to school, better is to listen to what his parents have been telling him and what his doctor too, advised. This is when he realized his mistake. He called his parents and said, "I am sorry for not listening to you, please help me to gain good health and I promise both of you to do whatever you ask me to do."

His parents helped him gain his mobility by giving him healthy food and helping him do small exercises regularly. Soon he started going to school. All his friends again started talking to him and playing with him. They also started helping him gain good health by playing with him regularly. He always ate healthy food no matter how difficult it seemed to him. He was determined to do it. He never troubled his maid aunty for junk food anymore. He watched T.V. for a very short time each day.

He actually started explaining the importance of good health to whoever he met. He completely changed himself. Since he started feeling very light and energetic from within and could do so many new things which he earlier used to avoid or could not do.

Rompo was now living a new active life. He loved his new version.

MY LEARNING

Listening to the experience of Rompo, from my best friend, even I started exercising regularly and tried eating healthy food. I always ate what my mother gave me to eat. I also told Rompo's story to my friends and cousins to motivate them to remain healthy.

MORAL

Appropriate exercise and diet is a key to good health.

11.

ONE TRUE FRIEND CAN MAKE A LOT OF DIFFERENCE

Ravi was a brilliant student in my class. He used to come first in class most of the time. He was a very sensitive boy and generous too. He would go up to everyone and be friends with them.

Everyone in my class pretended to be their friends as he used to bring chocolates everyday and give them off to his friends. My classmates used to be very good to him for the chocolates but used to speak bad about him when he was not there. One would say, "Who would like to be Ravi's friend, he cannot even speak properly." The other one would say, "I am his friend only for the tasty chocolates. I don't like him because he is every teacher's favourite. He seems fake to me."The one and only problem with Ravi was his speech. He used to stammer.

He used to participate in all the competitions other than the competitions related to speaking. Children used to make fun of him. He was not a good friend of mine but, I always used to tell my friends not to make fun of him and that he is a good boy.

A new boy named Roshan joined our class. Roshan was also good at studies. He soon became Ravi's friend. Both of them used to study and play together. They were both fond of each other. Roshan respected Ravi for his goodness to everyone.

One day, Roshan gathered courage and asked Ravi, "Do you know that your classmates don't like you? They just pretend to be your friends." Ravi said, "Yes, I know." "Then why are you good to them or share your things with them? Why do you give away all your chocolates to them? asked Roshan.

Ravi politely said, "I consider them to be my friends, it is up to them if they wish to be my friend or not." He further said, "I know that none of them will be good to me if I do not give them chocolates. They make fun of me because I stammer. This is my weakness." Roshan felt very sad listening to his friend's plead. His respect for Ravi increased from that time onwards.

Roshan did not like anyone making fun of his friend Ravi. He wanted all the students to genuinely like Ravi, what if God has not blessed him with a normal speech. No one is perfect. He thought of doing something for his friend.

One day, he made a list of all the classmates. As Roshan was liked by everyone and was friends with everyone. He secretly started approaching all his classmates asking the weakness of the other fellow students. It took him one week to complete that list.

One said, "Sunita always lies to her parents regarding homework." The other said, "Soju never takes care of his books they are all torn." One student said, "Roonam cannot even sing properly, she just pretends to be a good singer." Another said, "Uma has got a very bad hand-writing."

Like this he made a list of the weaknesses of his fellow classmates.

After he was satisfied with his work, Roshan approached his class teacher and told her everything. He said, "Ma'am I want to talk to my classmates regarding this and make them realize that not only Ravi, but everyone has got some or the other weakness. I want everyone to realise this and stop making fun of Ravi."

The teacher saw the efforts taken by Roshan to help his friend Ravi. The teacher appreciated the effort taken by Roshan and agreed to help him do what he wanted.

She could see his sincerity for this cause. Moreover, the students would learn something good for a lifetime.

She promised Roshan to give him sometime the next day when she comes to their class.

Next day the class teacher announced in the class, "Children, your friend Roshan wants to talk to all of you, please listen to him carefully." Everyone was surprised but sat attentively to listen to him.

Roshan thanked his teacher and started, "I am here to make friends with all of you by giving a small message of kindness which is hidden in my conversation with you all." We all were in suspense and started looking at each other. Roshan said pointing towards Roonam, "Roonam, you cannot sing properly, you just pretend to be a good singer." He then pointed towards Sunita saying, "Sunita, you always lie to your parents regarding your homework, Soju you never take care of your books, they are all torn. Uma your handwriting is very bad." etc. etc.

Everyone wondered how Roshan came to know all this. Before anybody stood up to argue with Roshan, he said, "I know you must be surprised to know how did I come to know all these things as I am a newcomer in the class." He went on saying, "My friends, my hidden message is that all of us have some or the other weakness just like Ravi. We should never make fun of anybody's weakness. It is quite possible that the next day someone would start making fun of our weaknesses too. We should always encourage and motivate our friends and stay united."

This gesture of Roshan made everyone realize their mistake. The entire class stood up to applaud for his efforts and the way he made all of us realize our mistake. We all thanked Roshan of thinking something like this and being a true friend to Ravi. The entire class started loving Ravi and never made fun of him again. Slowly Ravi even stopped bringing chocolates everyday. We all started caring for each other. We also learnt the lesson of true friendship from Roshan.

MY LEARNING

I still remember the way Roshan helped the class by reminding us of our weakness. He taught us how to help each other and stay united. This helped us to learn to accept and respect the other person along-with his weaknesses. We must support and help others to overcome their weakness. I also learnt the lesson of true friendship from him. This helped me to know that no one is flawless. We should actually encourage each other to overcome our shortcomings.

MORAL

Be a true friend.

THANKYOU

Thank you for reading these stories my little champs.

You have a whole new world to explore and contribute your bit to make your life and the life of your loved ones beautiful.

Hope you liked my contribution into your life. This is my drop in the beautiful ocean called life.

Live it well and stay blessed.

'JUVENILE PARABLES' Book-2 will be on your desk soon.

Stay   connected!!!!!

www.ingramcontent.com/pod-product-compliance
Lightning Source LLC
Chambersburg PA
CBHW031224160726
47992CB00006B/2880